OUR SOLAR SYSTEM

SEYMOUR SIMON

Updated Edition

HARPER

An Imprint of HarperCollins*Publishers*

To the kids who are science geeks and nerds
(like me) and enjoy reading about space

For a moment of night we have a glimpse of ourselves and of our world islanded in its stream of stars . . . voyaging between horizons across the eternal seas of space and time.

—Henry Beston
The Outermost House

Special thanks to Emily Stewart Lakdawalla

PHOTO AND ART CREDITS

Pages 4, 11, 13, 27, 28, 32, 38, 41, 44: NASA/JPL; pages 6, 46: NASA; page 7: ESA/NASA/SOHO; page 9: NASA/JPL/Ted Stryk/Gordan Ugarkovic/Mattias Malmer/Emily Lakdawalla; page 10: NASA/Johns Hopkins University Applied Physics Laboratory/Carnegie Institution of Washington; page 15: NASA/JPL and the Apollo 17 crew; page 16: Ann Neumann; page 17: NASA Goddard MODIS Rapid Response; page 19: NASA/GSFC/METI/ERSDAC/JAROS and U.S./Japan ASTER Science Team; page 20: NASA, J. Bell (Cornell U.), and M. Wolff (SSI); page 23: NASA/JPL/Cornell; page 24: NASA/JPL/University of Arizona; page 29: NASA/JPL/DLR; page 30: NASA/JPL/Space Science Institute; page 34: NASA, ESA, and M. Showalter (SETI Institute); page 36: NASA/JPL/Ted Stryk; page 40: NASA/JPL/Emily Lakdawalla; page 43: Dr. R. Albrecht, ESA/ESO Space Telescope European Coordinating Facility/NASA

ISBN 978-0-06-233379-7 (trade bdg.) — ISBN 978-0-06-114010-5 (pbk.)

14 15 16 17 18   SCP   10 9 8 7 6 5 4 3 2 1

❖

Revised Edition, 2014

Author's Note

From a young age, I was interested in animals, space, my surroundings—all the natural sciences. When I was a teenager, I became the president of a nationwide junior astronomy club with a thousand members. After college, I became a classroom teacher for nearly twenty-five years while also writing articles and books for children on science and nature even before I became a full-time writer. My experience as a teacher gives me the ability to understand how to reach my young readers and get them interested in the world around us.

I've written more than 250 books, and I've thought a lot about different ways to encourage interest in the natural world, as well as how to show the joys of nonfiction. When I write, I use comparisons to help explain unfamiliar ideas, complex concepts, and impossibly large numbers. I try to engage your senses and imagination to set the scene and to make science fun. For example, in *Penguins*, I emphasize the playful nature of these creatures on the very first page by mentioning how penguins excel at swimming and diving. I use strong verbs to enhance understanding. I make use of descriptive detail and ask questions that anticipate what you may be thinking (sometimes right at the start of the book).

Many of my books are photo-essays, which use extraordinary photographs to amplify and expand the text, creating different and engaging ways of exploring nonfiction. You'll also find a glossary, an index, and website and research recommendations in most of my books, which make them ideal for enhancing your reading and learning experience. As William Blake wrote in his poem, I want my readers "to see a world in a grain of sand, / And a heaven in a wild flower, / Hold infinity in the palm of your hand, / And eternity in an hour."

Seymour Simon

MERCURY EARTH

MARS

VENUS

URANUS

JUPITER

SUN

SATURN

NEPTUNE

PLUTO

Our Solar System was born among the billions of stars in the **Milky Way** galaxy. About 4.6 billion years ago, a huge cloud of dust and **hydrogen** gas floating at the edges of the galaxy began to pull together to form a disk. The particles at the center of the disk packed more and more tightly together into a globe, becoming hotter and hotter. Finally, the enormous heat in the center of the globe set off a chain of **nuclear** explosions, and the sun began to shine.

The blazing sun blasted the nearby gases away. As the particles in the disk began to cool, they clumped together into rocky or icy masses called planetesimals. These masses became the rest of the Solar System: **planets**, moons, asteroids, meteoroids, and comets.

The sun is just an ordinary star among the 100 to 400 billion stars in the Milky Way galaxy. It is not the biggest or the brightest. But the sun is the star nearest to Earth and the center of our Solar System.

Eight planets travel around the sun in paths called orbits. Mercury, Venus, Earth, and Mars are called the inner planets. These four rocky planets are much smaller than the four giant outer planets—Jupiter, Saturn, Uranus, and Neptune—which are made mostly of gases. Six of the planets, including Earth, have moons circling around them.

Thousands of dwarf, or small, planets, such as Pluto, Eris, Haumea, and Makemake, orbit the sun beyond Neptune. Thousands of asteroids, such as Ceres, Pallas, and Vesta, orbit the sun between Mars and Jupiter. Comets and some asteroids cross the orbits of the planets.

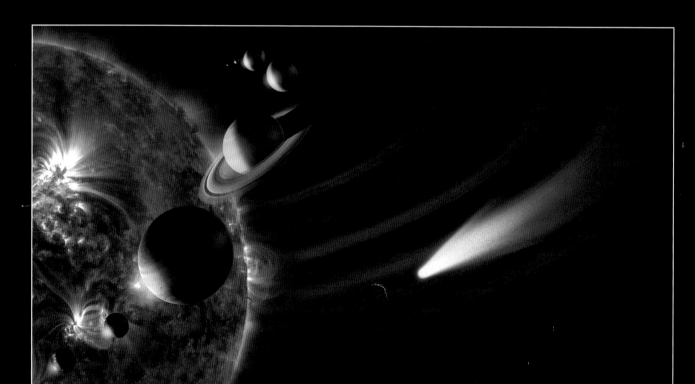

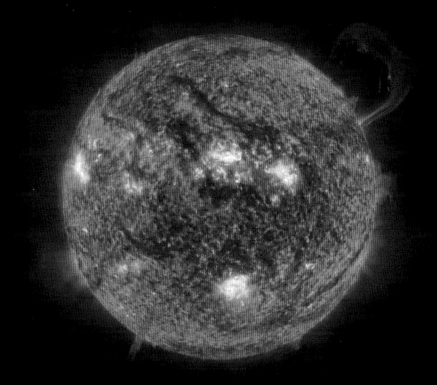

The sun is huge compared to Earth. If the sun were hollow, it could hold 1.3 *million* Earths. If Earth were the size of a basketball, the sun would be as big as a basketball court. In fact, the sun is about six hundred times bigger than all the planets, moons, asteroids, comets, and meteoroids in the Solar System put together.

Hydrogen is the sun's fuel. The sun uses about four million tons of hydrogen every second. Still, the sun has enough hydrogen to continue shining for another five to six billion years.

The sun is all-important to life on Earth. Green plants need sunlight to grow. Animals eat plants for food, and people need animals and plants to live. Our weather and climate depend on the sun. Without the sun, there would be no heat, no light, no clouds, no rain—no living thing on Earth.

Mercury is the closest planet to the sun. It was named by the Romans after their quick-footed messenger god. Mercury revolves quickly around the sun but rotates very slowly on its **axis**, so a day on Mercury is almost as long as two months on Earth.

Mercury is the smallest planet in our Solar System. Mercury is much smaller than Earth. In fact, it is smaller than Jupiter's and Saturn's largest moons. Mercury has no moons.

Mercury is often hard to spot because it is close to the sun's bright glare. It is visible to the naked eye during some early evenings or early mornings when the sun is below the horizon. When Mercury is viewed from Earth through a **telescope**, it appears to change its shape from day to day, similar to our moon.

MERCURY

VENUS

IO
(Jupiter)

EUROPA
(Jupiter)

GANYMEDE
(Jupiter)

CALLISTO
(Jupiter)

EARTH

MARS

TITAN
(Saturn)

MOON
(Earth)

TRITON
(Neptune)

The surface of Mercury has many craters, like on our moon. The larger craters were made by countless meteorites or asteroids crashing into the surface, which is not protected by an atmosphere. Unlike on our moon, most of Mercury's craters have flat floors. They were filled with volcanic lava billions of years ago.

Mercury is an almost airless planet. The temperature rises above 800 degrees **Fahrenheit** during the day, hot enough to melt lead. Yet during the long nights, with no atmosphere to trap the heat, the temperature on the dark side drops to –300°F, colder than Earth's South Pole.

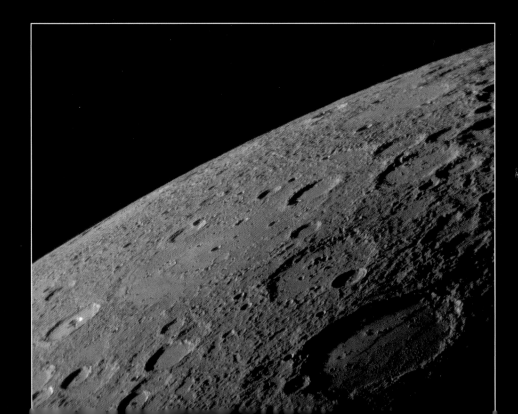

After our moon, Venus is the brightest object in the night sky. The Romans named Venus after their goddess of love and beauty. Venus is sometimes called the Evening Star or the Morning Star. But Venus is not a star. It is the second planet from the sun, between Mercury and Earth. Venus rotates from east to west, the opposite of most other planets and moons in the Solar System. Venus has no moons.

Venus is sometimes called Earth's sister planet because they are about the same size. But Venus is very different from Earth. Like Earth, Venus is covered by thick layers of clouds. But there is very little water on Venus, so the clouds around it are not made of water but of droplets of **sulfuric acid**.

Venus is the hottest planet in the Solar System, a desert with temperatures of close to 900°F. Sunlight passes through the atmosphere and heats the rocky surface. The rocks radiate heat, and the atmosphere traps the heat so it can't escape. This is called the greenhouse effect because the glass windows in a greenhouse act in the same way.

NASA's *Magellan* spacecraft orbited and photographed Venus for four years. On October 11, 1994, it made a dramatic conclusion to its highly successful mission by crash-landing in order to gain data on the planet's dense atmosphere and on the performance of the spacecraft. *Magellan* had radar-mapped 98 percent of the surface. It used a special kind of radar that shows details down to the size of a football field, with ten times the clarity of any previous photos.

This global view of the surface of Venus was computer-produced by *Magellan*'s mapping. Venus has large craters but no small ones. That's because the planet's atmosphere is so dense that it stops smaller incoming meteors before they can hit the ground and make a crater.

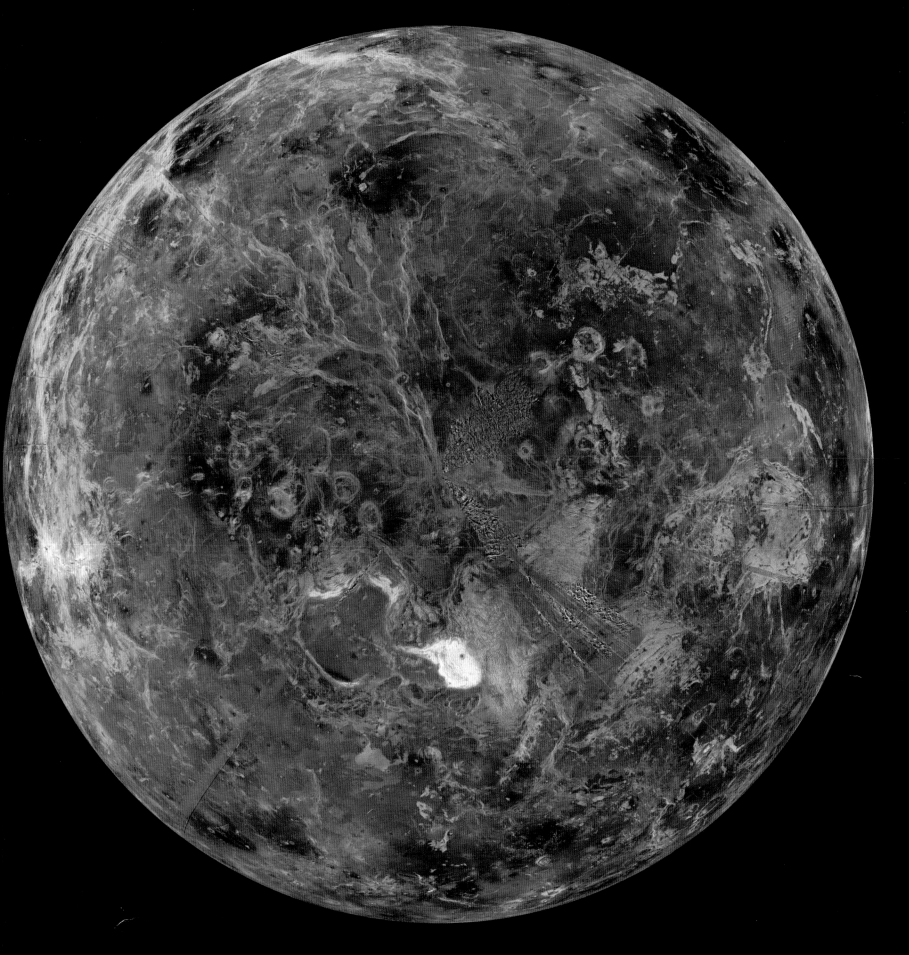

Earth might have been named Oceans or Water. Earth is the only planet in the Solar System with large amounts of liquid water on its surface and in its atmosphere. Earth is the third planet from the sun. If the sun were much closer, the seas on Earth would boil away. If the sun were farther away, the water would freeze over. The sun is just the right distance for life to exist on Earth. As far as we know, Earth is the only planet where there are living things.

This photograph of Earth from space was taken by the Apollo 17 astronauts as they left Earth on a mission to the moon. The brown places are land and the dark-blue places are oceans. The white clouds are part of Earth's atmosphere.

Earth is larger than Mercury, Venus, and Mars but much smaller than Jupiter, Saturn, Uranus, and Neptune. From space, Earth looks like a perfect ball. In fact, Earth is about twenty-seven miles wider at the equator than at the poles. As it orbits the sun, Earth spins like a giant top. One complete spin is called a day.

Earth is tilted a little to one side as it travels around the sun. For part of the year, the northern half of Earth has summer because it is tilted toward the sun and gets more direct rays of sunlight for a longer part of the day. During that time, the southern half is tilted away, so it has winter. As Earth continues to orbit, the southern half tilts toward the sun and has summer, while the northern half tilts away and has winter.

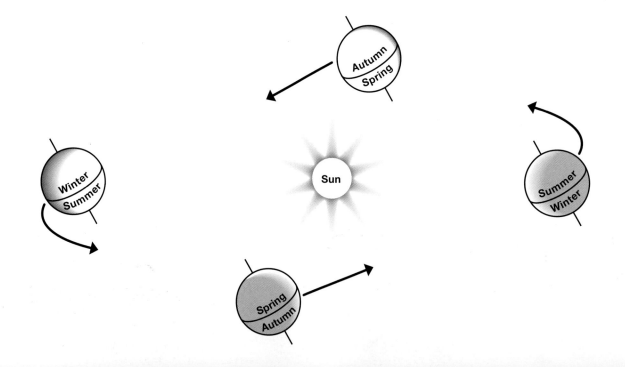

Earth is surrounded by an atmosphere, which helps keep the temperature fairly steady. The atmosphere is made up mostly of the gases nitrogen and oxygen, along with a small amount of **carbon dioxide** and tiny particles of dust and water. We live at the bottom of the atmosphere in a five- to ten-mile layer of air called the troposphere. Most weather takes place in the troposphere. The photo shows the spinning clouds and the eye of a typhoon in the troposphere over the Pacific Ocean.

Earth is covered by a layer of rocks called the crust, which ranges from 5 to 30 miles deep. The solid crust sits on the mantle, an 1,800-mile-thick layer of heavy rock. The mantle is very hot, so it flows very slowly, even though it's not melted. The crust is broken into a number of huge pieces called plates. The plates move on the slowly flowing mantle. Volcanoes erupt and earthquakes shake the land where the plates crash against each other, such as along the rim of the Pacific Ocean.

Earth's crust is constantly changing. This is a photograph of a mountainous area in the western United States. Mountains are pushed up by pressures within the Earth. Cracks in the rocks, called faults, run through the crust. The rocks also wear away. Gravel washes down from the tops of mountains into the valleys below. In the winter, ice breaks up rocks. People also change the land by farming or by shifting the course of rivers to provide water. They dig for rocks and minerals and use them to build roads and cities.

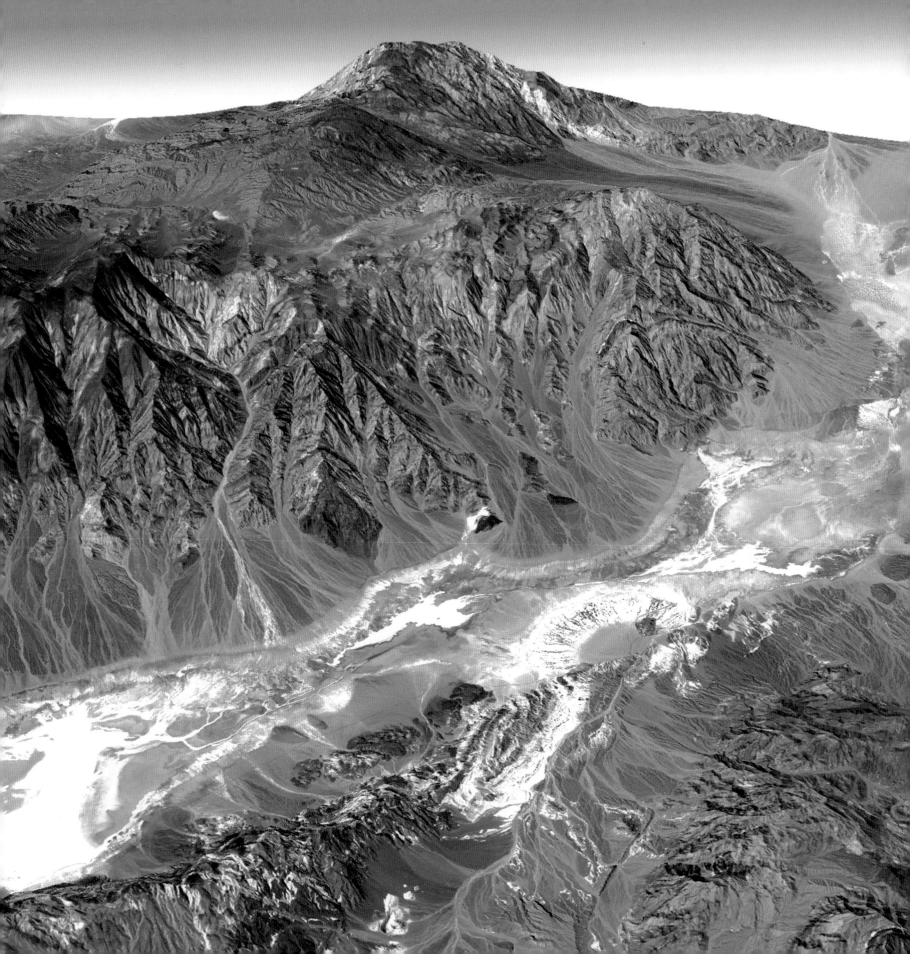

Mars is the fourth planet from the sun. It appears so bright in the night sky because it is closer to us than any other planet except Venus. Because it appears reddish, it reminded the Romans of blood, and they named the planet after their god of war.

People once imagined that Mars was covered by straight, dark lines. They thought that these lines were giant canals built by intelligent Martians. The idea of intelligent life on Mars was dispelled long ago, and in the 1970s, robotic spacecraft from Earth first reached Mars. This view of Mars was taken by the Hubble Space Telescope. It shows the southern polar ice cap on Mars. The Martian polar caps are composed mostly of frozen water, just like Earth's polar ice caps. But in winter, the poles get so cold that carbon dioxide freezes out of the atmosphere and makes the winter cap bigger.

The surface of Mars is covered by orange-red, dusty soil, which is blown about by the wind in the very cold, thin atmosphere. The orange-red color is due to the chemical compound in the soil and rocks. Millions of years ago, when Mars was a young planet, water flowed on the surface. Lots of water ice is buried just below the surface across Mars's northern hemisphere. In 2008, the *Phoenix* lander touched down near Mars's north pole. It used a scoop to dig into the ground and uncovered water ice.

Earth has sent more missions to Mars than to any other planet. We have mapped the whole planet with orbiters such as *Mars Express* and *Mars Odyssey*. Rovers such as *Spirit*, *Opportunity*, and *Curiosity* have rolled across the surface, photographing and analyzing rocks, soil, and weather. This information has helped scientists to make many important discoveries. They think that Mars was once much more like Earth is now, with oceans and rivers and a thicker atmosphere.

Jupiter is the giant planet of the Solar System, more than one and a half times as big as all the other planets put together. If Jupiter were hollow, more than 1,300 planet Earths could fit inside. Jupiter is the fifth planet from the sun and was named after the ruler of the Roman gods.

Jupiter is a gas planet made up of hydrogen and **helium**, covered by constantly moving clouds hundreds of miles thick. Jupiter's white clouds are made of frozen ammonia crystals. Scientists don't yet know for sure what gives the red clouds their color.

One of the many mysteries on Jupiter is a giant windstorm called the Great Red Spot. The spot is nearly two times the size of Earth. It was first seen through a telescope more than three hundred years ago. At different times, it has shrunk or grown, turned dull pink or bright red. But it has kept the same oval shape for centuries. Once in a while it meets and merges with smaller storms.

One of the *Voyager* spacecraft's most exciting discoveries was that Jupiter has rings circling the planet. The photograph (right) was taken by the *Galileo* spacecraft in 1996 and shows Jupiter's rings. All the four giant outer planets—Jupiter, Saturn, Uranus, and Neptune—have rings.

Jupiter is unlike Earth in many ways. The temperature at the cloud tops is very cold—more than 250°F below freezing. Its surface is an ocean of liquid hydrogen that may be ten thousand or more miles deep. At its center, Jupiter is very hot. The heat from below stirs up the liquid hydrogen and the cloud tops so that they rise and sink. Life as we know it could not exist on Jupiter. Jupiter and the other outer planets are strange and unfamiliar places that we have only begun to explore.

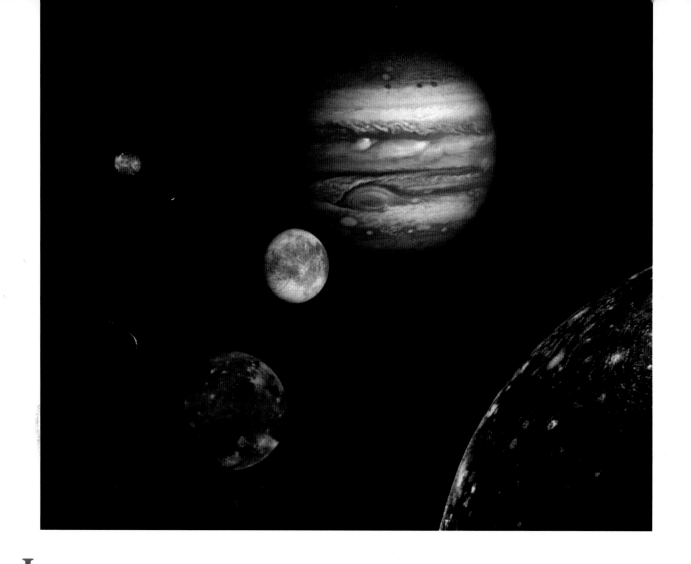

Jupiter has more known moons than any other planet in the Solar System. Jupiter has four major moons and at least sixty-three minor ones. The four largest moons are named Io, Europa, Ganymede, and Callisto. These are called the Galilean moons, after Galileo, the great scientist who discovered them in 1610 with his small homemade telescope. The minor moons are small. Most are less than fifty miles across and have odd shapes. Many of these are thought to be asteroids that were captured by Jupiter's strong **gravity**.

Spacecraft such as *Galileo* have given us close-up looks at the moons of Jupiter. Ganymede is the biggest moon in the Solar System, larger than the planet Mercury. Callisto is ancient, covered with impact craters like our moon.

Europa (both images below) is about the size of Earth's moon. It has a frozen crust on top of a cold, saltwater ocean. Scientists think there may be hot-water vents at the bottom of Europa's ocean, just as on Earth. Because of the salty, chemical-rich ocean, Europa is one place in the Solar System where there could be microscopic life.

Io has something that no other moon in the Solar System has: exploding volcanoes. The volcanoes erupt molten lava that cools to make rock, just as on Earth. But away from the volcanoes, Io is very cold. Sulfurous chemicals freeze at the surface, making Io's colorful frosts.

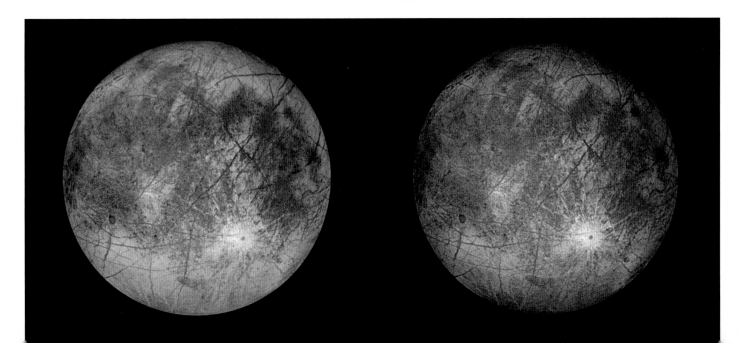

Saturn is the second-largest planet after Jupiter. If Saturn were hollow, about 750 planet Earths could fit inside. Like Jupiter, Saturn is a gas planet made up mostly of hydrogen and helium. Saturn is the sixth planet from the sun and was named after the Roman god of farming.

Galileo looked at Saturn through his low-power telescope nearly four centuries ago. He was shocked to see what looked like ears on either side of the planet. Galileo decided that they were two smaller globes. About fifty years later, the astronomer Cassini looked through a stronger telescope and saw that the two globes were really a flat ring around the planet.

Even if you look through a powerful telescope on Earth, Saturn appears to have just a few rings. But spacecraft photos, like this one by the *Cassini* orbiter, show that the large rings are made of thousands of smaller rings. If you were to get closer, you would see that the rings are made of pieces of ice. Some are as small as a fingernail; others, as big as a house. The rings also contain dust and bits of rock. And all the materials in the rings spin around Saturn like millions of tiny moons.

The rings are nearly 17,000 miles across but are less than 3 miles thick, and some are even thinner. How did the rings form? Some scientists think that the rings around the gas planets contain materials left over when the planets formed. Perhaps pieces of nearby moons that were chipped off by incoming meteorites helped to form rings. No one knows for sure.

Saturn has one large moon and six medium-sized moons among its fifty-six **satellites**. Most of Saturn's moons are ice covered and marked with craters.

This picture of Saturn and some of its moons was made from a number of photographs taken by *Voyager 1*. Saturn is partly hidden by the moon Dione. Enceladus and Rhea are off in the distance to the upper left. Tethys and Mimas are off to the lower right. Titan, Saturn's largest moon, is far away at the top right. Titan is bigger than the planet Mercury. In 2006, the *Cassini* spacecraft discovered that Enceladus is shooting out a giant plume of water vapor. The discovery has led scientists to believe this moon of Saturn might have a liquid sea under its icy surface.

Titan is the only moon in the Solar System known to have an atmosphere. On January 14, 2005, the European Space Agency's *Huygens* probe reached the upper layer of Titan's atmosphere and landed on the surface after a parachute descent of two hours and twenty-eight minutes. The probe found that Titan has river valleys that look like Earth's—except Titan's rivers contain liquid **methane**, not water.

Uranus is the seventh planet from the sun. Years after its discovery by William Herschel through a telescope in 1781, the planet was named Uranus after the Greek god of heaven and ruler of the world. Uranus is a ringed planet made up mostly of gases, about halfway in size between Jupiter and Earth. If Uranus were hollow, about fifty planet Earths could fit inside.

In January 1986, the *Voyager 2* spacecraft swept past the blue-gray clouds of Uranus. Uranus is tipped on its side in space. When *Voyager 2* passed by, Uranus's south pole was pointing at the sun, in the middle of forty-two years of constant sunlight. Uranus looked boring, with no obvious clouds. Since the 1990s, we have watched Uranus go through a change of seasons with the Hubble Space Telescope. As spring came to the northern hemisphere, Uranus's atmosphere developed clouds and storms just like the other giant planets.

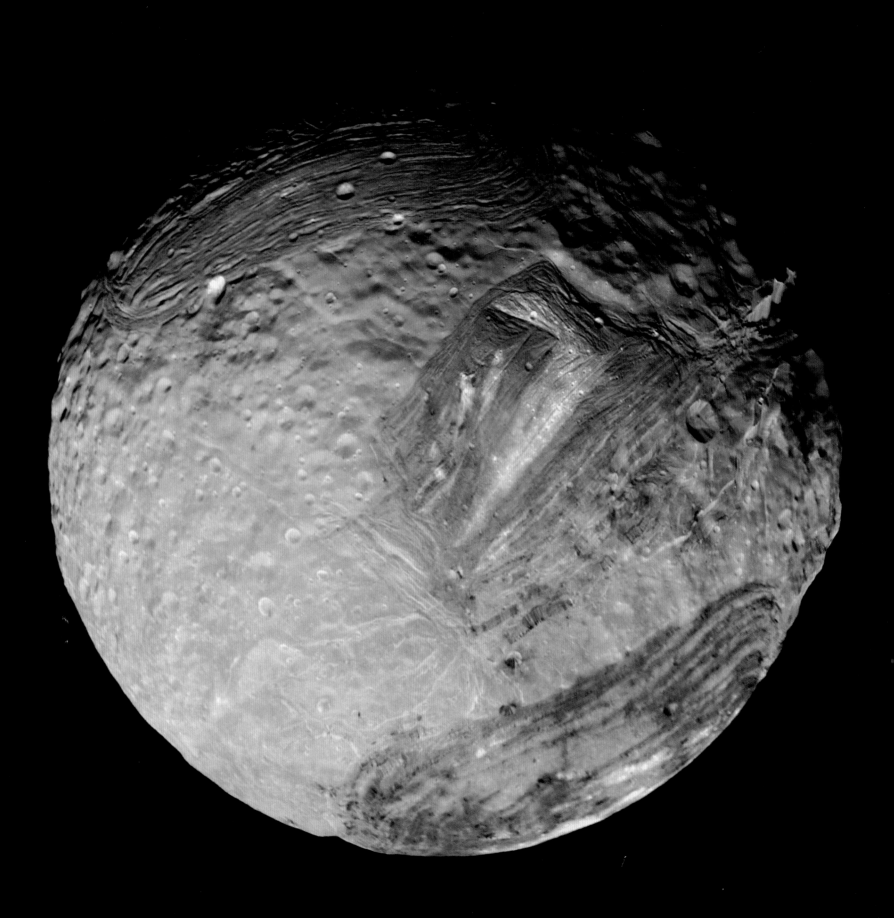

Uranus has five large moons and at least twenty-two smaller ones. Many of the smaller moons are icy and have strange surface features. This view shows part of Miranda, innermost of the five larger moons. Miranda is the most unusual of the moons. Huge canyons, deep grooves, ridges, and ropelike markings cover its surface—all this on a moon only three hundred miles across.

Uranus has eleven thin rings, along with pieces or arcs of other rings. The rings are made of chunks of an unknown black material that spins around Uranus like lumps of coal on a merry-go-round.

Neptune is too far from Earth to be seen without a telescope. Galileo saw Neptune through his small telescope but mistook it for a star. It was first identified as a planet in 1846. Later it was named Neptune, after the Roman god of the sea. Neptune is just a bit smaller than Uranus.

Neptune is a ringed gas planet with dark storms, giant hurricanes, and streaky white clouds of methane ice that float thirty-five miles above the lower cloud deck. When *Voyager 2* passed by, it saw one storm, the Great Dark Spot, that was bigger than Earth. More recent Hubble images show that the Great Dark Spot has now vanished. Strong, frigid winds in the atmosphere blow at the fastest speeds ever measured on a planet, up to seven hundred miles per hour. Methane in the atmosphere absorbs the red light from the sun but reflects the blue light back into space. This is why Neptune is blue.

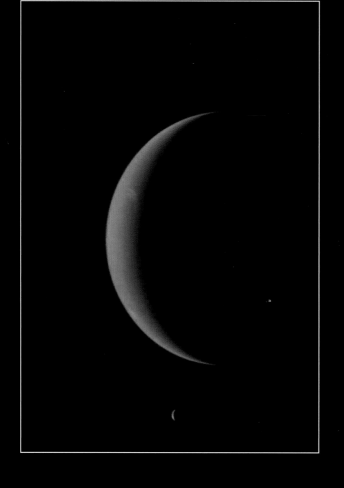

Twelve years and more than 2.8 billion miles after leaving Earth, *Voyager 2* whizzed past Neptune on August 25, 1989, and headed on its way out of the Solar System. The spacecraft found that Neptune has two bright outer rings, a fainter inner ring, and a thin ring of dusty material. At the time of this writing, there are no missions planned to return to Uranus or Neptune.

"A world unlike any other" is how scientists described Neptune's moon Triton. Neptune has at least thirteen moons, two large ones and eleven smaller ones. Triton is the biggest, about 1,700 miles across, nearly the same size as our own moon. Triton is colder than any other object ever measured in the Solar System. Large parts of the satellite look like the rind of an orange, with gigantic cracks running across the surface. Triton has a strange orbit—backward compared to the direction in which Neptune rotates. Scientists think Triton was originally a **Kuiper Belt** object, like Pluto, captured by Neptune's gravity.

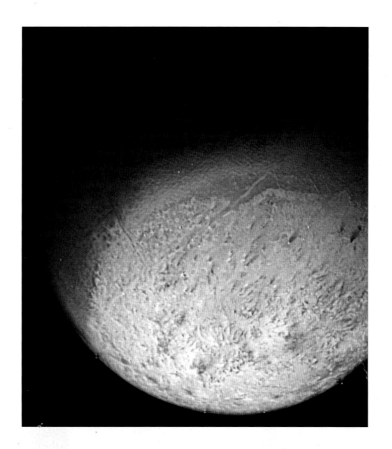

Discovered in 1930, Pluto had remained undetected for many years because it is so far from Earth and less than two-thirds the size of Earth's moon. Pluto was named after the Greek and Roman god of the underworld. It was long thought to be the smallest, coldest planet of our Solar System.

In 1978, astronomers discovered that tiny Pluto has a large moon of its own and named it Charon, after the boatman on the river Styx in the underworld. Charon's diameter is slightly more than half of Pluto's. Charon revolves close to Pluto and speeds through its orbit in only six days and nine hours. This is a photo (facing page) of Pluto (left) and Charon (right).

Scientists now use three ways to classify a planet: 1. It must orbit the sun. 2. It must be big enough for gravity to squeeze the planet into the shape of a basketball. 3. The planet must clear other smaller rocky or icy bodies out of its way when it orbits around the sun.

In 2006, scientists decided that Pluto should not be called a planet at all since it cannot clear bodies as it is orbiting the sun. This third rule of planet classification is what demoted Pluto from

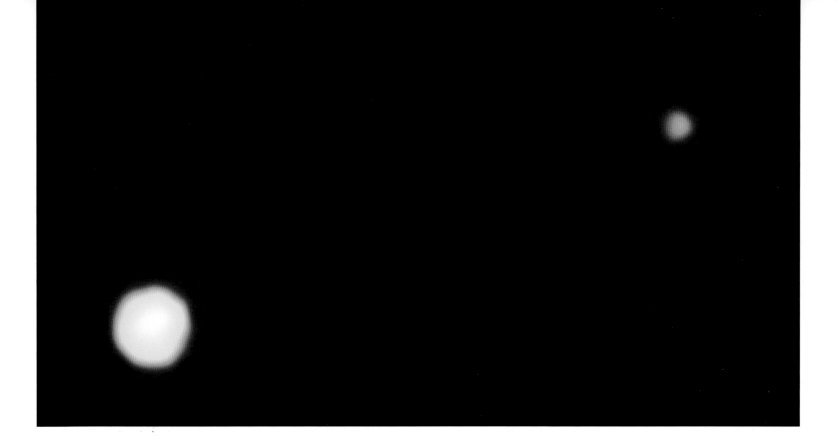

planet status to dwarf planet. A dwarf planet only has to be round and orbit the sun. Pluto is one of the largest of a group of icy balls of frozen rocks and gases that exist far beyond the orbit of Neptune in a region called the Kuiper Belt.

For now, the dwarf, or smaller, planets include Pluto; Ceres, the largest asteroid; Eris; Quaoar; Varuna; Ixion; Orcus; Haumea; and Makemake. Discovered in 2003, Eris is larger than Pluto and orbits in the Kuiper Belt far beyond Neptune. But there are dozens more dwarf planets in the Kuiper Belt, scientists say. Who knows what other new discoveries scientists will make about the Solar System?

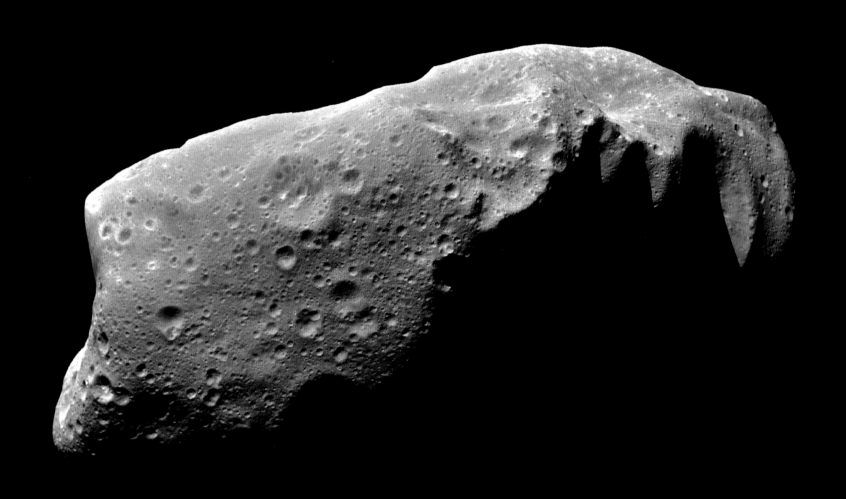

Asteroids are very small worlds that circle the sun, mainly between the orbits of Mars and Jupiter, a region called the asteroid belt. There are millions of asteroids, and more are discovered every day.

Sometimes called minor planets, all the asteroids combined would not make a world as large as our moon. Most are only a few miles across. Ceres, about six hundred miles in diameter, is by far the largest asteroid. Pallas and Vesta are the next largest asteroids, both more than three hundred miles in diameter.

Some asteroids have orbits that cross Earth's. Every day, tiny asteroids burn up in our atmosphere, making meteors. Bigger asteroids may explode in the atmosphere, making fireballs. Chunks of an asteroid that fall onto the ground are called meteorites. Some asteroids are large enough to cause major disasters if they hit Earth. One such asteroid likely caused the dinosaurs to die out. More recently, on February 15, 2013, an asteroid entered Earth's atmosphere over a town in Russia named Chelyabinsk. Fortunately, the asteroid exploded in the air without reaching the ground. The shock wave from the explosion damaged buildings, but if the asteroid had hit the ground, the damage would have been much worse. It was the largest known asteroid impact in the last one hundred years. Scientists are working hard to find all the large asteroids before they hit us, but the Chelyabinsk asteroid was too small to detect.

Comets orbit the sun, but they are quite unlike planets. When a comet approaches Earth, it may look spectacular, with a long, glowing tail stretching far across the sky. But comets don't always look like that.

When a comet sweeps in toward the sun, it begins to change. The pressure of sunlight and streams of particles from the sun sweep dust off the comet's surface and evaporate some of the ice. The dust and gas begin to glow and form first a halo, called the coma, and then finally a tail, which may stretch for millions of miles.

Around a dozen "new" comets are discovered each year. Most come from the region of icy objects in the Kuiper Belt. Other comets, called long-period comets, arrive from an even more distant region in space called the Oort Cloud. These comets can take as long as thirty million years to complete one trip around the sun. Far from the sun, a comet is just a "dirty snowball," a frozen ball of ice a few miles wide covered by a layer of black dust.

Our bodies are made up from some of the same **atoms** that formed the sun and the stars and created the planets, moons, asteroids, comets, and meteoroids.

We are all part of the universe.

GLOSSARY

Atom—The smallest unit of all matter.

Axis—An imaginary straight line around which a body or geometric object rotates.

Carbon dioxide—A colorless, odorless, and nonflammable gas.

Fahrenheit—A temperature scale where water freezes at 32 degrees and boils at 212 degrees.

Gravity—The natural force of attraction applied by a celestial body, such as Earth, upon objects at or near its surface.

Helium—A colorless, odorless, gaseous element occurring in natural gas.

Hydrogen—A colorless, highly flammable gas, the lightest of all gases; it is the most abundant element in the universe.

Kuiper Belt—A region filled with icy objects in our Solar System, similar to the asteroid belt.

Meteoroids—Small pieces of metal or rock that may have been swept off asteroids or comets.

Methane—An odorless, colorless, and flammable gas.

Milky Way—The galaxy containing our Solar System that can be seen as a band of light stretching across the night sky.

Nuclear—The release of massive amounts of energy at the atomic level.

Planet—A large, celestial body that moves around, and is lit by, the sun.

Satellite—A celestial body that orbits a planet; for example, Earth's moon.

Sulfuric acid—A dense and oily liquid formed when water and sulfur dioxide mix with oxygen.

Telescope—An arrangement of lenses and mirrors that allows people to see very distant objects.

READ MORE ABOUT IT

Smithsonian Institution
www.si.edu

National Aeronautics and
Space Administration
www.nasa.gov

Jet Propulsion Laboratory
www.jpl.nasa.gov

The Hubble Space
Telescope website
www.hubblesite.org